I Am ₙₒₜ Very

BRAVE

Timothy Knapman and Gavin Scott

bookoli

There was once a little dragon called Boggle. Boggle wanted to be like his hero,

SUPERDRAGON!

But Boggle was NOT very brave. He was afraid of everything.

Heights.

Noises.

Vegetables.

And most of all ...

NEW THINGS.

There was an
especially big New Thing headed his way ...

... DRAGON SCHOOL!

It was far away, on the other side of a very high bridge.

"Superdragon would walk across this bridge," said Daddy.
"But Superdragon is super brave," said Boggle.

"I am not very brave."

But Boggle knew he had to try.

So he shut his eyes tight, thought about Superdragon and walked across the bridge, holding on to Daddy's hand.

When they reached school,
Boggle could hear dragons playing.

They sounded really **big** and **loud.**

Welcome to
DRAGON SCHOOL

"Superdragon would make lots of
nice friends here," said Daddy.
"But Superdragon is super brave," said Boggle.

"I am not very brave."

But Boggle knew he had to try.

So he shut his eyes and thought about
SUPERDRAGON.

Superdragon would have gone to school with

super BIG and
super SCARY dragons.

"Oh no..." thought Boggle.

Class 1B

But he
couldn't stop now.
He took a deep breath,
put on his hero's mask
that he'd brought just in case,
and jumped into the class shouting,

"I am ...

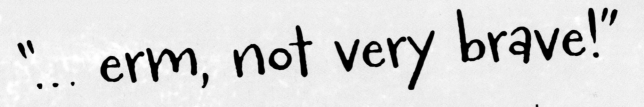

"... erm, not very brave!"

But then he looked around.

All the other dragons were little.

And none of them looked brave either,

because the first lesson was ...

... FLYING!

Boggle was afraid of heights.

But he knew he had to try.

He thought about Superdragon,

flapped his wings...

... and rose higher and higher off the ground.

Boggle thought flying would be scary.

And strange.

But it was WONDERFUL!

At hometime, Boggle told his daddy all the things he'd done that day.

"But you always say you're not very brave," smiled Daddy.

"I am not VERY brave, Daddy ...

"... I am SUPER brave!"